Franklin Benjamin Hough

Papers concerning the Attack on Hatfield and Deerfield by a Party of Indians from Canada, September Nineteenth, 1677

Anatiposi

Franklin Benjamin Hough

Papers concerning the Attack on Hatfield and Deerfield by a Party of Indians from Canada, September Nineteenth, 1677

Reprint of the original.

1st Edition 2023 | ISBN: 978-3-38230-295-5

Anatiposi Verlag is an imprint of Outlook Verlagsgesellschaft mbH.

Verlag (Publisher): Outlook Verlag GmbH, Zeilweg 44, 60439 Frankfurt, Deutschland
Vertretungsberechtigt (Authorized to represent): E. Roepke, Zeilweg 44, 60439 Frankfurt, Deutschland
Druck (Print): Books on Demand GmbH, In de Tarpen 42, 22848 Norderstedt, Deutschland

Bradford Club Series.

NUMBER ONE.

PAPERS

CONCERNING THE ATTACK

ON

HATFIELD AND DEERFIELD

BY

A PARTY OF INDIANS FROM CANADA

SEPTEMBER NINETEENTH

1677

NEW YORK
1859

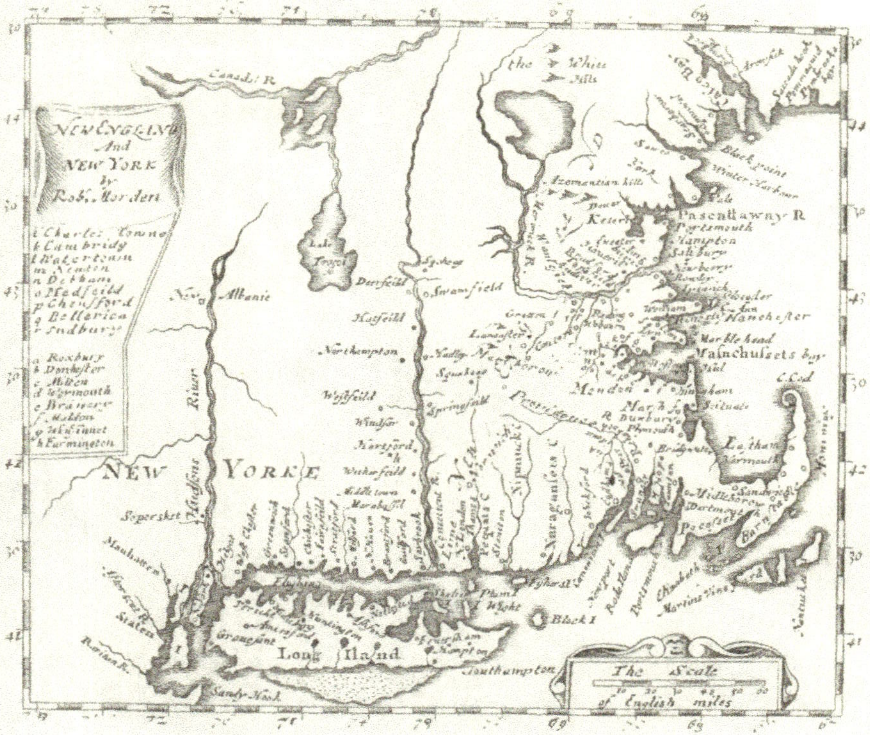
NEW ENGLAND And NEW YORK by Robt. Morden
NEW YORKE
Long Island
Masachusets bay
The Scale of English miles
Canada R
Hudsons River
Albanie
Black I
C. Cod
Nantucket

SUBSCRIBER'S COPY.

THE BRADFORD CLUB.

Under this designation, a few gentlemen interested in the study of American History and Literature, propose occasionally to print limited editions of such manuscripts and scarce pamphlets as may be deemed of value towards illustrating these subjects. They will seek to obtain for this purpose, unpublished journals or correspondence containing matter worthy of record, and which may not properly be included in the Historical Collections or Documentary Histories of the several states. Such unpretending cotemporary chronicles often throw precious light upon the motives of action, and the imperfectly narrated events of by-gone days; perhaps briefly touched upon in dry official documents.

The Club may also issue fac-similes of curious manuscripts, or documents worthy of notice, which like the printed issues will bear its imprint.

"These are the
Registers, the chronicles of the age
They were written in, and speak the truth of History
Better than a hundred of your printed
Communications."—*Shakerly Marmyon's Antiquary.*

William Bradford, the first New York Printer, whose name we have adopted, came to this country in 1682, and established his press in the neighborhood of Philadelphia. In 1693 he removed to this city, and set up the first press "at the sign of the Bible." His first work printed in this colony was entitled "The Laws and Acts of the General Assembly." During a period of thirty years, he was the only Printer in the Province, and in his imprints, he styled himself "Printer to the King." In 1725 he printed our first newspaper, "The New York Gazette." He continued the business of his profession until within a few years of his death, which occurred in 1752 at the age of 92 years. He was described in an obituary notice of the day as "a man of great sobriety and industry, a real friend to the poor and needy, and kind and affable to all."

APRIL, 1859.

PREFACE.

The papers contained in the following pages, are copied from the originals in the office of the Secretary of State, at Albany, and form a part of the archives of the colonial period of New York. The leading facts concerning the invasion of the Connecticut valley in the autumn of 1677, have since the time of their occurrence, been familiarly known through the published narrative of a prisoner, and the record of cotemporary writers.

The ravages of a hundred and eighty years have, however, consigned to oblivion many of the details connected with that event, so widely and generally reported in the community and generation in which it occurred; the hand of time is gradually obliterating the written memorials of that day, and oral tradition has long since distorted into fable, if not entirely lost, the exact statements of those who witnessed the scenes and felt the sufferings which they described. Every document therefore, which was written upon the occasion, carries us back to the time, and spreads before us the circumstances of the event. We learn, as from the lips of a witness, the terror which the news of the sudden invasion spread through the community; we feel the painful suspense scarcely relieved by a ray of hope, concerning the dismal fate of the captives, and we share in the exultation with which the loved and the lost are restored to the bosoms of their families.

The papers forming the text of this volume, have never before been printed, and it is believed they will form an interesting contribution to the history of the times to which they relate.

F. B. H.

Albany, January 25, 1859.

INTRODUCTION.

Hatfield is situated upon the west bank of Connecticut river, about midway between the north and south bounds of the state of Massachusetts, and upon the northern border of Hampshire county. The settlement of this town was preceded by that of Hadley upon the opposite side of the river, and commenced nearly twenty years previous to the incursion detailed in the following pages. Its first settlers were six of the pioneers of Hadley, and for several years it was included within the corporate limits of that town. A considerable tract of land, embracing almost the whole of the northern meadow in the present town of Hatfield, was granted to Mr. Bradstreet and Major Dennison, and the conflict of this claim with those of the settlers of Hadley, led to a spirited declaration by the latter to the general court, but their efforts were not successful, and in 1664, agents were sent by that town to purchase the meadow of Mr. Bradstreet. The negotiation was successful, and the tract was purchased, excepting a reservation of one thousand acres, for the sum of two hundred pounds. The reservation was long denominated The Farms, but ultimately it was divided up and sold.

The settlement west of the river, had in a few years so increased, that a division of Hadley became necessary, and Hatfield was erected into a separate town on the 11th of May, 1670. Town officers were first chosen in the following year, and about the same time, liberty was granted by the Hampshire county court, "to enter into Church estate." The Rev. Hope Atherton, a graduate of Harvard college, became the first minister, and continued in the pastoral relation until his death in 1677, at the age of thirty-three, from disease contracted by exposure and hardship in the celebrated "Falls fight," in May, 1675. Hatfield purchased from the Indians in 1672, a tract adjoining on the north in the present town of Whately, paying fifty fathoms of wampum for the same. This town does not appear to have been represented in the general court until twenty years after its incorporation.[1]

Some idea may be formed of the relative importance of Hatfield at about the period under consideration, from the proportion which it paid of the colonial tax. This was as follows:[2]

	Colony.	Hatfield.
October 24, 1674,	£1,299 : 8 : 10	£10 : 17 : 2
do 13, 1675,	1,553 : 6 : 4	8 : 12 : 0
1675–6,	1,281 : 0 : 10	8 : 12 : 8

On the twentieth of January, 1687, the county tax upon Hadley and Hatfield was:

Upon Hadley,....................	£9 : 15 : 8
do Hatfield,....................	4 : 5 : 2

If these taxes were uniformly levied upon the whole

---

[1] *Holland's History of Western Massachusetts*, i, 69. Ed.

[2] *Coll. Am. Stat. Asso.*, i, 255. Ed.

property, this frontier town possessed considerably less than one per cent of the total wealth of the colony, and less than half of that in the parent town.

The danger of attack from hostile Indian tribes, had been early taught in the sad experience of many New England towns, and had led to the location of settlers in villages. Each family here possessed a small plot of ground for a garden, and owned an individual or common right in the fields devoted to cultivation. The villagers were accustomed, in times of danger, to labor in bands, and often went armed to their daily task. The social influences thus concentrated, and the conveniences thus afforded for schools and religious worship, have had doubtless their influence upon the New England character, while the many dangers with which they were environed, served to unite them more closely by mutual interests in the common welfare. While danger from Indian incursions existed, these villages were commonly surrounded by a line of stockades, which afforded protection against sudden attack, but unless judiciously defended, could not long resist a courageous enemy.

Hatfield had been the theatre of Indian warfare, before the event related in the following pages. In August, 1675, numbers of the Indians living upon the Connecticut river, began openly to evince their sympathies for the success of Philip of Mount Hope, then waging a war of extermination against the colonists. The boldness and success of his efforts, bespeak the force of his character, and the skill of his diplomacy, by which, uniting the discordant factions and allaying the petty jealousies of rival Indian tribes, he brought them to combine in a desperate effort for the eradication of the white race from their land.

Governor Hutchinson, and those who have followed

him, state that on fast day, September 1st, 1675, the settlers were suddenly attacked by a party of hostile Indians, who were repulsed with loss.

Barry, in his *History of Massachusetts*, adopts the account given by Hutchinson, and relates that as the savage war-whoop was ringing, and the confused and terror-stricken inhabitants were about seeking a slender chance of safety in flight, a man of military bearing and venerable age, suddenly appeared among them, and with sword in hand, and a voice accustomed to command, rallied the disordered crowd, and placing himself at their head, quickly restored their courage, turned the scale of victory, and compelled the Indians to retreat hastily with loss.

The unknown personage who had thus led them to victory, as suddenly disappeared, and many believed that an angel from heaven had come to their assistance. It was not known till near twenty years afterwards, that two of the judges who had condemned Charles the First to the block, were then concealed in Hadley, upon the opposite bank of the river, and there is little reason to doubt, but that William Goffe, who had served as a major-general in the armies of Cromwell, was this angel of deliverance.

Most of the historians of this period, relate this incident substantially as above given, but locate the event at *Hadley*, upon the occasion of its attack, on the 12th of June in the year following.[1]

---

[1] This event is not noticed by Hubbard, in his *History of the Indian Wars of New England*, published in 1677, and certified upon highly respectable authority as being accurate and reliable in all respects. It further appears that no general fast day was appointed on the above date. Compare *Barry's Hist. Mass* (colonial period), 420; *Hutchinson's Hist. Mass*, i, 201; *Hoyt's Indian Wars*, 135, 136; *Stiles's Hist. of the Three Judges*, 109, 110; *Holland's West. Mass.*, i, 128. ED.

Deerfield and Northfield soon after experienced severe reverses from the enemy, and Springfield became an object of vengeance, but although favored by the treachery of professedly friendly Indians, their plans were detected in season to prevent their full accomplishment.

The success of the Indians made them eager to finish the work of annihilation, and on the 19th of October, they again fell upon Hatfield, in great numbers. The place was garrisoned by Captains Moseley and Poole, while a body of troops was stationed at Hadley under Captain Appleton, and another at Northampton under Major Treat. The latter hastened to the assistance of their Hatfield friends, and the conflict, after a few hours of sharp fighting, was decided in favor of the settlers, the latter losing but about a dozen men, while the Indians had great numbers slain.[1] Hostilities continued in the Connecticut valley till near winter, and Deerfield having been mostly burned, was abandoned to the savages. A quantity of grain that was stacked in the fields, escaped destruction, and the commanding officer at Hadley, anxious to secure this supply, sent Captain Lathrop with a party of men, and a number of teams, to thresh the grain and bring it to head quarters. The labor was accomplished and the party were returning, when they were ambuscaded, on the 18th of September, by about seven hundred Indians, and the captain and seventy-six men were slain. The whole number in the party was eighty-four, of whom eighteen were teamsters. A monument of marble, about twenty feet in hight, was erected in

[1] *Hubbard's Indian War*, 43; *Mather*, 18; *Barry's Hist. Mass.* (colonial period), 422; *Holland's West. Mass.*, i, 105; *Drake's Hist. Boston*, 411.
ED.

August, 1838, to commemorate the locality of this melancholy disaster.[1]

The details of this campaign do not strictly come within our limits to notice. Philip, the controlling spirit of these movements, disappeared from the theater of action, and is supposed to have spent the winter in the vicinity of Albany; doubtless busy in extending disaffection among the Indians, and laying new plans for more extensive operations. The United Colonies of New England were also engaged in concerting measures and procuring means for effectually terminating the war.

Occasionally the murder of an unguarded person or family indicated the presence of lurking savages, and towards spring the upper settlements on the Connecticut again became the principal scene of warfare. The memorable swamp fight in South Kingston, Rhode Island, on the 18th of December, had broken the strength and crushed the hopes of the Indians in that quarter, and many of the Narragansetts fled westward to join in hostile operations, as occasion might favor.

Northampton was attacked early on the 14th of March, 1676, where several houses were burned, five persons killed, and several wounded. Repulsed from this place, they immediately went to Hatfield, but were prevented from attacking it by the fortunate arrival of troops from Hadley. They returned to Northampton the same day, but made no further attempt at that time.

In May, word was received that the Indians were planting at Deerfield, and fishing at the Great falls above that place, since known as Turner's falls. A plan of attack was devised, and executed with terrible

---

[1] *Barber's Hist. Coll Mass.*, 248; *Hoyt's Indian Wars*, 105. Ed.

effect. The enemy had no intimation of the approach of the English, until aroused from their morning slumbers by the roar of musketry. Many in their confusion rushed into the river and were swept over the falls; others perished in their cabins, and others who fled for shelter to the river bank, were slain without the power of resistance. The work of death went on until over three hundred Indian warriors perished, while the English lost but one man.[1] On their return, however, they fell into the hands of another body of Indians, and many of their number were killed, including Captain Turner, the leader of the expedition.

This event, which occurred on the 18th of May, 1676, was followed in twelve days by an attack upon Hatfield, by from six to seven hundred Indians. Almost every man was at work in the meadow, and the few that remained made a spirited resistance, but could not prevent the Indians from firing several of the buildings. With the assistance of a party from Hadley, who were attracted over by the smoke of the burning buildings, the enemy were finally repulsed, with a loss of twenty-five killed. Of the English, five men were killed, and three wounded. On the 12th of June, Hadley was attacked by a large body of Indians, who were repulsed with heavy loss, and this was the last engagement in the war in which the enemy appeared in numbers, or evinced their accustomed bravery.

The fortunes of Philip had tended rapidly downward since the fight at the falls; the Mohawks had become his active enemies, and his friends one by one were killed, or despairing of success yielded themselves to the mercies of the English. Retiring to his ancient

[1] *Hoyt's Indian Wars*, 129. ED.

seat at Mount Hope, with a few followers who remained true to his cause, he continued the unequal contest against fate, until at length, betrayed and hunted from his last remaining refuge, he was slain.

This important event occurred on the 12th of August, 1676, and was soon followed by a peace with all the New England tribes, by which the colonies were left to realize the severity of their losses, and repair the ravages of their wasted settlements.

It will be remembered, that during the whole of this war, the home governments of New England and Canada were at peace, and their American colonies were withheld by treaties from favoring hostile enterprises against each other. England had been at peace with France since 1668, and was not involved in war with that country until twelve years after the events related in these papers. The Count de Frontenac, then governor of Canada, had received instructions from his sovereign, Louis XIV, to cultivate a good understanding with the English, and avoid any cause of complaint.[1] Still the relations existing between the French in Canada and the English in New England and New York, were at no time cordial, and in the rivalry for the monopoly of the Indian fur trade which existed many years between New York and Canada, it not unfrequently happened that just causes of complaint arose upon both sides, and representations were made to the home government by each party, that the other had adopted unfair measures for securing the coveted profits of this trade, or were making dangerous alliances with the Indian tribes. In fact while these events were transpiring in New England, the French had their emissaries at the castles of the Five Nations,

[1] *New York Colonial Documents*, ix, 126, 128. Ed.

and were drawing large numbers, especially of the Mohawks, within their immediate influence, and settling them within sight of Montreal.

During the progress of Philip's war, intimations were at times received, that he was secretly supplied with arms and ammunition by the French in Canada, and the people of New York were publicly charged with selling powder to the enemy. This accusation was indignantly repelled by the governor and council of the colony, and a careful examination of the facts will satisfy every candid person that it was without foundation, unless perhaps in individual cases, in which mercenary dealers might have privately sold ammunition without being inquisitive as to its intended use. Stringent regulations against the practice were passed, and prosecutions for their alleged violation were promptly instituted.[1]

The Indian tribes had been nominally at peace with the English colonies of New England about a year previous to the attack upon Hatfield, to be hereafter more particularly described. The frontier settlers, deprived of everything but the soil, ventured to return to their wasted fields, and to reconstruct their dwellings; but still doubting the good faith of the Indians, they prudently kept watch, and usually went to their daily work and to their public meetings, with arms in their hands. There was reason to apprehend that the Indians who had fled to the French in Canada, would revisit their former haunts, and the subsequent inroads from that quarter, show that the spirit of revenge was long harbored against those who had deprived them of their lands, and driven them from the homes and

[1] *Narrative of the Causes which led to Philip's Indian Wars* (*Munsell's Hist. Series*), 114, 115, 122, 130, 136, 179. Ed.

graves of their fathers. It scarcely admits of doubt, but that this hostile feeling was favored and promoted by the French, with the design of securing the Indians more strongly to their interests. This policy lay at the foundation of the whole scheme of colonization, and was zealously and successfully prosecuted by them until their final conquest more than eighty years afterwards. The fact that the Indians found purchasers for their prisoners in Canada, indicates the light in which these incursions upon the English were regarded, if it does not afford an explanation of the motives which prompted them. A cherished feeling of revenge, or a morbid thirst for plunder, might have led these savages to fall upon exposed settlements, and destroy with the inhabitants such fruits of their labor as could not be appropriated to their wants, but we are led to attribute the preservation of prisoners, and their removal to Canada, to the hope of profits from their sale or redemption.

The settlement at Hatfield was suddenly attacked by a party of Indians, at about 11 o'clock in the morning, on the 19th of September, 1677, at a time when the inhabitants were wholly unconscious of danger, and most of the men at work raising a frame outside of the fortification. Three of their number were shot down before reaching the town, and the savages, breaking through the feeble defences of the village, killed eleven and took seventeen prisoners. Several buildings were burned, and the marauders departed, leaving six or seven of the settlers wounded.[1]

[1] The names of the killed were: Sergeant Isaac Graves, John Atchinson, John Cooper, the wife and child of Philip Russell, the wife and child of John Coleman, the wife of Samuel Kellogg, the wife and child of Samuel Belding, and a child of John Wells. Those taken captive

At about sunset the same day, they came upon Deerfield, whose inhabitants were also unprepared for resistance, and engaged in raising a house. One of four men who fled to a swamp was pursued and killed, and three other men were taken prisoners. The name of the former was John Root; the latter were, Sergeant John Plympton, Quintin Stockwell, and Benoni Stebbins.[1] After gathering such plunder as might be conveniently brought away, the savages withdrew, and took up their slow and painful march for the French settlements in Canada.

On the same day a party of Indians appeared upon the Merrimack, and persuaded or compelled Wonalancet of Waamkeke, a sachem of influence, and then supposed to be on friendly terms with the English, to leave with them for the north, from whence he never returned. The party that surprised Hatfield and Deerfield numbered about fifty Indians, under the command of Ashpelon, a chief whose name appears in history only in connection with this event. From the testimony of the prisoners, he appears to have been more humane than many whom he commanded, and that through his influence several of their number were saved from torture. It was at first supposed that the assailants were Mohawks, as a party of those Indians had passed through the place the day previous, with a number of friendly Indians as prisoners, and a scalp; but it was soon ascertained that the enemy were

---

were: two children of John Coleman, the wife and three children of Benjamin Waite, Mrs. Foote and two children, the wife and two children of Stephen Jennings, Obadiah Dickinson and one child, a child of Samuel Kellogg, a child of William Bartholomew, and a child of John Allis.—*Holland's Western Massachusetts*, i, 134. ED.

[1] *Ibid*, 135. ED.

from Canada, and probably some of those who had formerly lived in the Connecticut valley.[1]

The news of this incursion spread rapidly through the colony, and the remaining members of the broken families lost no time in endeavoring to ascertain the destination of the prisoners. Benjamin Waite, whose wife and children were among the captives, hastened to Albany, thinking that the assailants were Mohawks, but finding that they were not, he returned home. The report brought back by Stebbins, gave the first positive indication of the number and destination of the party, which was no sooner learned than a plan was arranged for visiting Canada, to recover their families and friends by ransom. In answer to a petition from Hatfield for aid in this enterprise, the general court, on the 22d of October, issued the following order for this purpose, and resolved that the expenses attending it should be defrayed by the colony.

"In answer to the petition of Hatfeild, & for the recouery of their captiues, the hono[r]d Gouerno[r] is

---

[1] A letter from Edward Rawson, secretary, dated October 22d, 1677, contains the following statement:

* * * * *

"About 3 weeks since (when we hoped to be at rest), a party of about thirty of the old enemy, viz, Hadley & Northampton Indians fell vnexpectedly vpon Hattefeild, burnt fouer houses, fower barnes, some stackes of corne, killed diuerse persons, and carried away one & twenty prisoners, men, weomen & children. One of the men escaped, and saith the Indians were gon vp Conecticot Riuer, northward, towards the French, from whence they came, & sajd they were incouraged and ffurnished for this attempt by a French Capt. Wee haue it vnder consideration to send to these Indians & to the French to endeavour the recouery of the poore captiues, & the better to vnderstand what wee may expect from those quarters." * * * * *

—*Records of Massachusetts*, v, 162. ED.

desired & empoured to take order & care therein, by granting comission to such meete persons as may be imployed in that service, & giving them instructions to mannage that affayre, and by them to write to the French gouno^r at Canada, as also to those Indians that haue the prisoners in possession, and make such ouertures to them as may tend to the regayning the prisoners & the setling of the peace of the country, & that the chardge thereof be borne by ye country."[1]

Another source of disquiet had about the same time occurred in the colony. The Mohawks had made a predatory incursion into Massachusetts, and fallen upon the Indian settlements of Natick and Hassenemesett, taking several captives and killing an inoffensive man. These Indians were settled under the protection of the English, professing faith in their religion, and a desire for improvements in the arts of civilized life. Six Mohawks had also been taken up while hunting in the vicinity of Charles river, and thrown into prison. An opportunity was thus offered for opening a correspondence with the New York Indians, through the government at Albany, with the view of restoring these Indian captives to their friends, preventing future occasion for complaint, and, if possible, of inducing the warlike Mohawks to pursue the hostile party then on their way to Canada, and rescue the prisoners with them. It would seem that war in some form was essential to the existence of these savages, who divided their time between the perils of the chase and hardships of distant journeys, to surprise the feeble and unsuspecting tribes of other colonies, to plunder their cabins, and lead off the miserable captives which they

---

[1] *Records of Massachusetts*, v, 168. ED.

took, for deliberate torture. The request of the Massachusetts people was conveyed to the Mohawks by the six Indians of that tribe then in prison, who were released and conducted safely beyond the settlements toward Albany.

In a letter dated on the 12th of October, 1677, and addressed to the Mohawks, after remonstrating against the attack upon their friendly Indians, and apologizing for having taken up six of their number near Boston, they added:

"There are other Indians for you to fall vpon, whose pursuing & destroying wee shall take kindly from your hand, namely, a parsell of Indians who came lately from Canada, and fell vpon Hattfeild, the same day when 4 of yor people lodged in Hatfeild, and were there kindly vsed the night before. These Indians, who came from Canada, as wee since came to know by one of our captives that is gott away from them, haue carrjed wth them twenty of our people, weomen & children, wth three men, whom we vnderstand are returning towards Canada. It would be an acceptable service to us, if yow cann destroy this parcell of Indians; and may yow be instrumentall for the sauing & recouering of any of our captives, wee shall giue yow good reward for the same."[1]

These six Mohawks were also the bearers of the following letter to the commandant at Albany:

"Capt. Salisbury.

S^{r}: Wee haue thought fit to acquaint yow, that sixe Indians by whom wee send these to yow, were some days since taken by some of our people wthin Boston

[1] *Records of Massachusetts*, v, 166; *N. Y. Coll. MSS.*, xxvi. ED.

bounds, on the northerly side of Charles River. It being a place where wee haue no Indians setled, or allowed to goe wthout speciall order from ourselues, they were forthwith carryed to prison, and being examined by authority, sajd they were Macquas, though wee had cause to doubt of it; yet, since being assured by some of Albany that they are reall Macques, wee haue given order for their enlargement & well vsage, and haue appointed sixe troopes to guard them & conduct them safe ^{x}into the woods out of our tounes, or hazards of our Indians, whom some Macques haue lately don injury vnto, carrying away captiues two of our Natick Indian weomen, and killing one very honest man of them & taking away his scalp, all which being contrary to their agreement wth them by our messingers in Aprill last. Wee might well haue secured some of these till sattisfaction made, and the returning of these two captiues; but to prevent all ground of disquiet to the Macqua sachem, wee haue, notwthstanding, set these at liberty, & make vse of them to signify our minds to the sachems, that they send home those squaes, whose returne from them wee doe expect, & there instructing of their men not to come into these parts to our friend Indians, which was one great end of our treating them at Albany in Aprill last. Though wee did then designe their falling on the eastern Indians, our then ennemjes, wherein they haue not don vs any service, yet wee did as strongly aime at, & as carefully prouide for the security of our friend Indians, wch they engaged to do, not to do them any mischeifes; and it is a great trouble to us that they or theire people take no more care thereof, wee being ingaged to protect & secure them, who in the tjme of the warr were very serviceable to vs, ventured their liues for us, & many of them lost their liues in our service; and now wee shall not let them be destroyed by either Macquas or others. Wee vnderstand that Majo^r Pinchon hath lately wrote to yow vpon the occasion of some mischiefe doun at Hatfeild as well as formerly, directing the Macquas to thake their randge more norward, that the Macquas would not adventure to come neere our tounes now, because the ennemy Indian hauing made an irruption vpon us, we are vpon our guard, and haue our scouts out, & so, not knouing Macquas from other Indians, there may be hazard of doing them hurt vnknoune, for wee cannot distinguish them, vnless some Englishman or Dutchman should come wth them, or some one of them might adventure into our tounes vnarmed, with a letter in his hand; otherwise wee know not how they will be safe. Wee pray yow so to informe the Macquas with it, that they may not come into any dainger; and doe us that favour to let the Macquas know how ready & willing we are to hold & continue all amicable correspondence & friendship with them, & therefore expect their attendance to their agreement wth us, not to doe spoyle vpon our friend Indians. Wee haue speciall respect for them, especially those of Naticke Pvncapawag & hereabouts, whom his Maj^ties Corporation [the Society for Propagating the Gospel in Foreign Parts] also hath lately manifested great respects for, so that it is hoped & expected that the Macquas will be very observant hereof for the future.

S^r wee further desire your helpfullness in recouering of those of our people who are now in captivity with the barbarous heathen, there being twenty persons taken from Hattfeild & Deerefeild, as Majo^r Pynchon hath given yow an account, desiring you to incite the Macquas to pursue the enemy, being Indians that came from the French, and are thither returning, as wee are certeinly informed by one of our men that escaped from them. Wee doubt not of yor readiness to affoord help, as it may fall in yor way, and you need not doubt of our care to sattisfy what charge yow may be at, and shall disburse vpon the account. Wth our loving respects to yew, wee comend yow to God, & are

Your assurd ffriends

EDW^{D} RAWSON, Secre$^{ty.}$

In the Name & by order of the Gen^{all} Court."[1]

The effort to arouse the Mohawks was not successful, nor did they cease to molest the Christian Indians of Massachusetts. In June of the following year, a rumor was reported at Albany, that two large war parties of these Indians were assembling near Schenectady, one of which it was suspected was about to invade Massachusetts. A troop of sixty Mohawks, under the command of Tahiadouson Tyados, arrived at Albany a few days after, having three men, fifteen women and four children, prisoners. They proved on examination, to be Natick Indians, friendly to the English, and under the care of Major Daniel Gookin. They had been surprised in a corn field called Magachnah on Magoneog, six miles from Sudbury, and were conducted by their captors into the Mohawk country. In a letter to Colonel Brockholls, acting governor, written a few days after, Captain Salisbury states his belief that these prisoners had since been mostly burnt, and that he could have released them for two hundred pounds, but had no orders for disbursing money for the Indians of other colonies. He soothed his conscience by the remark that if he had, "the governor would be angry, we having nothing to do with them,

[1] *Records of Mass.*, v, 166. ED.

nor receiving any profit by them, and with your leave my thoughts are, that if the New England people had any kindness for them, they would have sent a man in time enough to have been at Albany to have spoken to Tyndais."

It is proper to state, that this narrow policy did not meet the approbation of Colonel Brockholls, who in a letter of July 20th, in answer to the above, said:

* * * "It seems very strange that the peace between us should be held upon such unequal and tickelish terms, that notwithstanding we deal with them in all friendship, yet they shall presume to break it when they please, as now particularly their falling upon our neighbors' friendly Indians, contrary to their engagements, and expecting money for their delivery. They deserve rather to be checked for their insolence than to be soothed up in it. If they have such encouragement, their attempt may be upon Christians, so that they may be paid for their ransom. I suppose that consideration hindered the New England men from sending money." * * * * *

Samuel Ely and Benjamin Waite were soon after commissioned to visit Albany, and take such measures as might be possible for the restoration of the Indian prisoners. Furnished with a commission from Governor Leverett, and a letter from Major Pynchon, and attended by Peter De Vos, a Dutch interpreter, and two Natick Indians, they proceeded to Albany and were allowed by Captain Salisbury to pass to the Mohawk's country.

An interview was obtained at Albany, and the grievance and claims of the agents were stated. To this the Indians replied, by acknowledging the kind offices they had received from New England people, and excused the attack upon Magoneog by the plea that their young warriors when abroad were like wolves, and that the Indians they attacked were not dwelling as friendly Indians near the English plantations, but in the woods, and in a castle well fortified by stockadoes. They reminded the agents that their discourse had been made without giving presents, as was the invariable custom upon such occasions, and promised to restore the surviving captives. Their speech was concluded as follows:

"Upon this following proposition we can not forbear (according to our custom) but give a small present, though of little value, being a fathom of zewant [wampum].

BRETHREN: The covenant that was made here last year betwixt Major Pynchon and us, in the presence of the governor general, is as fast, firm and inviolable as ever it was, and if our warring against the Indians of the north in general doth not please you, pray acquaint us here therewith.

They do repeat again, that the covenant made with the brethren, is as firm as ever it hath been, and do present some zewant made round as a circle, which they compare to the sun, saying that their alliance is as firm and inviolable as the sun, and shall have such a splendor as the beams thereof, and say furthermore, that if any will speak with them, that this is the appointed place, as they of Maryland have done, and that in the governor general's presence.

BRETHREN: There is a troop or two of our Indians out against your and our enemies, who know nothing of this, and if they should come to your habitations, let not them be kept fast, or any harm done to them, and if they should take away any of your friend Indians, there shall be no harm done to them, but restored again to any person you shall commission to receive the same with the rest, provided our governor general be present."

Captain Salisbury was severely censured by the acting governor, for allowing a conference to be held with the Mohawks by the agents of another colony, in his absence. We have stated this affair somewhat in detail, as illustrative of the temper of the times, the relations which the Mohawks sustained towards the governments of New York and Massachusetts, and the jealousy with which the former regarded the slightest interference by any other colony with Indian affairs within its borders. It is probable that this difficulty between the Mohawks and the Christian Indians of Massachusetts, arose from the neglect or refusal of the latter to pay tribute to the former, as had been for some time their custom. Similar incursions were made upon the Mohegans of Connecticut, for the avowed purpose of compelling them to keep up their payments to the powerful and warlike lords of the Mohawk valley.

The journey of Waite and Jennings to Canada, for the recovery of the Hatfield prisoners—begun on the verge of winter, and leading through regions then almost unknown to the English—was an enterprise involving great hardship and peril, and nothing short of the object then pressing, could have induced them to undertake it. Mr. Waite was joined by Stephen Jennings, whose wife and children were also among the prisoners, and having completed their arrangements, they set out upon their errand of love on the 24th of October, 1677.

They had provided themselves with a commission and letters from the governor and other persons in Massachusetts, directed to the authorities at Albany and in Canada, explaining their mission and bespeaking assistance and favor in promoting its object. They reached Albany on the seventh day, and delivered their message to the commandant at that place, but there is sufficient reason to infer that they were not received in the spirit that persons under their circumstances might expect from a humane and civilized officer, speaking their language and professing allegiance to the same sovereign authority.

Captain Salisbury, the commanding officer, appears to have been avaricious, jealous, and arbitrary to an extent happily uncommon, and instead of promoting the object of their journey, evidently wished to oppose obstacles to its performance.[1] The travelers were ordered not to leave town without again calling upon this personage, perhaps again to meet another postponement of their business; but the urgency of the case permitted of no delay, and without complying with the order, they continued their journey, passing over to Schenectady, seventeen miles westward, to obtain the services of an Indian guide, as the route they were to travel was mostly unknown to the whites, and communication with the French had as much as possible been cut off by the regulations of the government.

The Dutch of Schenectady, upon enquiring of them their business, were told *that they belonged to Boston.* As

---

[1] Captain Sylvester Salisbury was appointed commandant at Albany on the 14th of May, 1670, in place of Captain John Baker, who had held this office from the month of August, 1668, but who was dismissed from all military service at Albany or elsewhere, upon the appointment of his successor.—*Council Minutes*, iii, 27. ED.

they understood the language but imperfectly, these people took this assertion to signify that the town of Schenectady formed a part of the Boston colony, instead of the simple and obvious meaning that the travelers themselves belonged to that government. Considering this heresy too dangerous to tolerate, they caused them to be sent back to Albany, where they were detained as prisoners until a favorable opportunity occurred for sending them to New York to answer for their treason before the governor and council.

They appeared before the council on the 10th of November, and the nature of their mission and cause of detention being explained, they were dismissed, with an order that no hindrance should be again permitted within the jurisdiction of the colony. They returned to Albany on the 19th of November, where they tarried till the 10th of December, waiting for ice to form on the northern lakes, that would greatly favor their journey. Securing with some difficulty an Indian guide on whom they could rely, they proceeded to Lake George, where finding a canoe, they crossed to the outlet of that lake in three days, and carried their craft two miles across the portage to Lake Champlain, which they reached on the 16th of December. The ice had not yet formed sufficiently to support them, and after trying to advance in this manner, they returned after one day's journey, and carried their canoe forward to the open waters of the lake. Here they were windbound six days, and unable to make any progress. Their provisions meanwhile became exhausted, and had they not killed some raccoons in a hollow tree near the shore, they would have suffered the utmost extremity of want.

On their way, they found a bag of biscuit and some brandy, in a deserted wigwam, that had probably been left by a Canadian or Indian hunter, and at length arrived at the frontier town of Chambly, then a settlement of ten houses, on the 6th of January. They found Jennings's wife on their way to Sorel, and five others of the captives at that place, several of whom had been pawned to the French by the Indians, for liquor. They learned that the remaining prisoners were with the Indians not far distant, excepting a little daughter of Mrs. Foote, and a child of Jennings, who had been put to death by the savages, the latter after their arrival in Canada. Mrs. Waite had added one to the number of captives soon after reaching their destination, and Serjeant Plympton of Deerfield had been burnt at the stake near Chambly. His fellow captive, Dickinson of Hatfield, had been compelled to lead him to his terrible death.[1] From the surviving prisoners they learned the details of the hardships of the march, and the harrowing scenes and worse forebodings that this band of women and children had witnessed and felt. During the whole of this period they were in imminent danger and constant fear of suffering the worst tortures that capricious and wanton savages could inflict; with which they were repeatedly threatened, and which they had witnessed upon the person of an aged man who had been their fellow prisoner.

They were often on the point of starvation, and towards the close of the journey, were exposed to the rigors of a northern winter. About two hundred miles above Northfield, the party had divided and crossed over to Lake Champlain, arriving, after intense suffering, at the frontier settlements of the French.

[1] *Holland's West. Mass.*, i, 135; *Hubbard's Gen. Hist. N. E.* (*Mass. Hist. Coll.*), 2d series, v, vi, 638.

Messrs. Waite and Jennings found it necessary to secure the assistance of the French governor to obtain the prisoners, and accordingly pushed on to Quebec, where they were kindly received and assisted in getting the surviving captives together. They were ransomed from the Indians by the payment of two hundred pounds, but remained in Canada until the approach of spring.

The cruel sufferings of the captive train, which was over three months on the painful journey, have been detailed in the following narrative of Quintin Stockwell, one of the prisoners:[1]

"It can not be altogether impertinent, but may discover much of the temper and management of the Indians in this war, to insert an account of one Stockwell, of Deerfield, concerning his captivity and redemption, with other notable occurrences during his continuance among them, written with his own hand, and are as follows, in his own words, viz:

September 19, 1677.—About sunset I and another man being together, the Indians with great shouting and shooting came upon us, and some other of the English hard by, at which we ran to a swamp for refuge, which they perceiving, made after us, and shot at us, three guns being discharged by me; the swamp being mirie, I slipt in, and fell down; whereupon an Indian stept to me, with his hatchet lifted up to knock me on the head, supposing I was wounded, and unfit for travel. It happened I had a pistol in my pocket, which (though uncharged) I presented to him, who

[1] This narrative was originally published by Dr. Increase Mather, in 1684. It is here given as found in *Blome's Present State of His Majestie's Isles and Territories in America* (1687), pp. 221–232. ED.

presently stept back, and told me if I would yield I should have no hurt, boasting falsely, that they had destroyed all Hatfield, and that the woods were full of Indians; whereupon I yielded myself, and fell into the enemie's hands, and by three of them was led away to the place whence I first fled; where two other Indians came running to us, and one lifting up the but-end of his gun to knock me on the head, the other with his hand put by the blow, and said I was his friend.

I was now near my own house, which the Indians burnt last year, and I was about to build up again, and there I had some hopes to escape from them; there was a horse just by, which they bid me take; I did so, but attempted no escape, because the beast was dull and slow, and I thought they would send me to take my own horses, which they did, but they were so frighted, that I could not come near them, and so fell again into the enemie's hands, who now took me, bound me, and led me away. Soon after I was brought to other captives, who were that day taken at Hatfield, which moved two contrary passions; joy, to have company; and sorrow, that we were in that miserable condition: We were all pinion'd and led away in the night over the mountains, in dark and hideous ways. About four miles further, before we took up our place of rest, which was a dismal place of a wood on the east side of that mountain; we were kept bound all that night, the Indians watching us, who, as they travell'd, made strange noises, as of wolves, owls, and other birds and beasts, that they might not lose one another; and if followed, might not be discovered by the English.

About break of day we marched again, and got over the great river Pecomptuck [Deerfield]; there the

Indians marcked out upon trays, the number of their captives and slain, as their manner is. Here I was again in great danger, a quarrel arising whose captive I was, and I was afraid I must be killed to end the controversie; they then asked me whose I was, I said three Indians took me; so they agreed to have all a share in me: I had now three masters, but the chief was he that first laid hands on me, which happened to be the worst of the company, as Ashpelon the Indian captain told me, who was always very kind to me, and a great comfort to the English. In this place they gave us victuals which they had brought away from the English, and ten men were again sent out for more plunder, some of whom brought provisions, others corn out of the meadows, upon horses; from hence we went up above the Falls, where we crost that river again, when I fell down-right lame of my old wounds received in the war; but the apprehension of being killed by the Indians, and what cruel death they would put me to, soon frightened away my pain, and I was very brisk again. We had eleven horses in that company, which carried burthens and the women; we travell'd up the river till night, and then took up our lodgings in a dismal place, being laid on our backs and staked down, in which posture we lay many nights together; the manner was, our arms and legs being stretched out, were staked fast down, and a cord being put about our necks, so that we could not possibly stir; the first night (being much tired) I slept as comfortably as ever; the next we lay in the Saquahog meadows [Northfield]; our provision was soon spent, and whilst we were there, the Indians went a hunting, and the English army came out after us. Then the Indians moved again, dividing themselves and the captives into many companies, that the English might not follow their track; at night, having crossed the river, we met again at the place appointed; the next day we repassed it, where we continued a long time, which being about thirty miles above Squag, the Indians were quite out of fear of the English, but much afraid of the Mohawks, another sort of Indians, enemies to them.

In this place they built a strong wigwam, and had a great daunce, as they call'd it, where it was concluded to burn three of us; having provided bark for that purpose, of whom (as I heard afterwards) I was to be one, Serjeant Plumpton another, and the wife of Benjamin Wait the third: I knew not then who they were, yet I understood so much of their language, that I perceived some were designed thereto; that night I could not sleep for fear of the next day's work, the Indians (weary with dancing) lay down and slept soundly.

The English were all loose, whereupon I went out for wood, and mended the fire, making a noise on purpose, but none awaked; I thought if any of the English should wake, we might kill them all sleeping; to which end I removed out of the way all the guns and hatchets, but my heart failing, I put all these where they were again. The day (when they intended to burn us) our master and some others spoke for us, and the evil was prevented at this time: We lay here about three weeks, where I had a shirt brought me to make; one Indian said it should be made this way, another a different way, and a third this way, whereupon I told them I would make it according to my chief master's order; upon this an Indian struck me on the face with his fist, I suddenly rose in anger to return it again, which raised a great hubbub; the Indians and English coming about me, I was fain to humble myself to my master, which ended the matter. Before I came to this place, my three masters were gone a hunting, and I was left with only one Indian (all the company being upon a march) who fell sick, so that I was fain to carry his gun and hatchet, whereby I had opportunity to have despatched him, but did not, because the English captives had engaged the contrary to each other, since if one should run away, it would much endanger the remainder: Whilst we were here, Benjamin [Benoni] Stebbins, going with some Indians to Wachuset Hills, made his escape, the tydings whereof caused us all to be called in and bound. One of the Indians captains, and always our great friend, met me coming in, and told me Stebbins was run away, and the Indians spoke of burning us; some were only for burning our fingers, and then biting them off; he said there would be a court, and all would speak their minds, but he would speak last and declare, that the Indian who suffered Stebbins to make his escape, was only in fault; and bid us not fear any hurt should happen to us, and so it prov'd accordingly.

Whilst we lingered here-about, Provision grew scarce, one bear's foot must serve five of us a whole day; we began to eat horse-flesh and devoured several horses, three only being left alive. At this time the Indians had fallen upon Hadley, where some of them being taken, were released, upon promise of meeting the English on such a plain to make further terms: Captain Ashpalon was much for it, but the sachins of Wachuset, when they came, were against it; yet were willing to meet the English, only to fall upon and destroy them. Ashpalon charged us English not to speak a word of this, since mischief would come of it. With these Indians from Wachuset, there came above fourscore squaws, or women and children, who reported the English had taken Uncas and all his men, and sent them beyond the seas; whereat they were much enraged, asking us if it were true; we deny'd it, which made Ashpalon angry, saying he would no longer believe Englishmen. They then examined every one apart; and dealt worse with us for a time, than before; still provision was scarse; at length we came to a place called Suavo-Maug-River, where we hoped to find salmon, but came too late; this place I reckon two hundred miles above Deerfield, then we parted into two companies, some went one way, and some another; we passed over a mighty mountain, being eight days in travelling of it, though we marched very hard, and had every day either snow or rain; we observed that on this mountain all the water ran northward. Here we likewise wanted provision, at length we got over and came near a lake, where we staid a great while to make canoes, wherein to pass over. Here I was frozen, and here again we were like to starve; all the Indians went a hunting, but could get nothing several days; they pawawed or conjured, but to no purpose; then they desired the English to pray, confessing they could do nothing, and would have us try what the Englishman's God could do: I prayed, so did serjeant Plumpton in another place, the Indians reverently attending morning and night; next day they killed some bears, then they would needs make us desire a blessing, and return thanks at meals; but after a while they grew weary of it, and the sachem forbid us: When I was frozen, they were very cruel to me, because I could not do as at other times.

When we came to the lake, we were again sadly streightned for provision, and forced to eat touch-wood fried in bear's grease; at last we found a company of racoons, and then we made a feast, the custom being that we must eat all; I perceived I had too much for one time, which an Indian that sate by observing, bid me to slip away some to him under his coat, and he would hide it for me till another time; this Indian, as soon as he had got my meat, stood up and made a speech to the rest, discovering what I had done, whereat they were very angry, and cut me another piece, forcing me to drink racoon's grease, which made me sick and vomit; I told them I had enough, after which they would give me no more, but still told me I had racoon enough, whereby I suffered much, and (being frozen) was in great pain, sleeping but little, and yet must do my task that was set me; as they came to the lake, they killed a great moose, staying there till it was all eaten, and then entered upon the lake; a storm arose, which endangered us all, but at last we got to an island, and there the Indians went to pawawing or conjuring; the pawaw declared, that Benjamin Wait and another were coming, and that storm was raised to cast them away: This afterwards appeared to be true, though then I believed it not; upon this island we lay still several days, and then set out again, but a storm took us, so that we continued to and fro upon certain islands about three weeks; we had no provisions but racoons, that the Indians themselves were afraid of being starved; they would give me nothing, whereby I was several days without victuals: At length we went upon the lake on the ice, having a little slead, upon which we drew our loads; before noon I tired, and just then the Indians met with some Frenchmen: One of the Indians who took me, came and called me all manner of ill names, throwing me on my back; I told him I could do no more, then he said he must kill me, which I thought he was about to do, for pulling out his knife, he cut off my pockets and wrapt them about my face, and then he helped me up, and took my slead, and went away, giving me a bit of biscuit like a walnut, which he had of the Frenchman, and told me he would give me a pipe of tobacco; when my slead was gone I ran after him (but being tired), soon fell to a foot-pace, whereby the Indians were out of sight; I followed as well as I could, having many falls upon the ice; at length I was so spent, I had not strength enough to rise again, but crept to a tree that lay along, upon which I continued all the cold night, it being very sharp weather.

I now counted no other but I must here die, which whilst I was ruminating of, an Indian hollowed, and I answered; he came to me and called me bad names, telling me if I would not go, he must knock me on the head; I told him he must then do so, he saw how I had wallowed in the snow, but could not rise; hereupon he wrapt me in his coat, and going back, sent two Indians with a slead; one said he must knock me on the head, the other said no, they would carry me away and burn me; then they bid me stir my instep, to see if that were frozen, I did so; when they saw that, they said there was a chirurgeon with the French that could cure me; then they took me upon a slead and carried me to the fire, making much of me, pulling off my wet and wrapping me in dry cloaths, laying me on a good bed; they had killed an otter, and gave me some of the broth, and a bit of the flesh; here I slept till towards day, and was then able to get up and put on my cloaths; one of the Indians awaked, and seeing me go, shouted, as rejoycing at it. As soon as it was light, I and Samuel Russel went afore on the ice upon a river, they said I must go on foot as much as I could for fear of freezing; Russel slipt into the river with one foot, the Indians called him back and dried his stockins, and sent us away with an Indian guide; we went four or five miles before the rest of the Indians overtook us; I was pretty well spent, Russel said he was faint, and wondred how I could live, for he said he had had ten meals to my one; I was then laid on the slead, and they ran away with me on the ice; the rest and Russel came softly after, whose face I never after saw more, nor knew what became of him. About midnight we got near Shamblee [Chambly], a French town, where the river was open; when I came to travel, I was not able, whereupon an Indian who staid with me would carry me a few rods, and then I would go as many, telling me I would die if he did not carry me, and I must tell the English how kind he was.

When we came to the first house there was no inhabitants; the Indian and I were both spent and discouraged, he said we must now both die; at last he left me alone, and got to another house, from whence came some French and Indians, who brought me in; the French were very kind, putting my hands and feet in cold water, and gave me a dram of brandy, and a little hasty-pudding and milk; when I tasted victuals, I was very hungry, but they would not suffer me to eat too much; I lay by the fire with the Indians that night, yet could not sleep for pain; next morning the Indians and French fell out about me, the Indians saying that the French loved the English better than the Indians. The French presently turned the Indians out of doors, being very careful of me, and all the men in the town came to see me: Here I continued three or four days, and was invited from one house to another, receiving much civility from a young man, who let me lie in his bed, and would have bought me, but the Indians demanded a hundred pounds; we travelled to a place called Surril [Sorel], whither this young man accompanied me to prevent my being abused by the Indians; he carried me on the ice one day's journey, for now I could not go at all; when we came to the place the people were kind.

Next day being in much pain; I asked the Indians to carry me to the chirurgeon, as they had promised; whereat they were very angry, one taking up his gun to knock me down, but the French would not suffer it, falling upon them and kicking them out of doors; we went away from thence to a place two or three miles of, where the Indians had wigwams; some of them knew me and seemed to pity me: While I was here, which was three or four days, the French came to see me, and (it being Christmas time) they brought me cakes and other provisions; the Indians tried to cure me, but could not; then I asked for the chirurgeon, at which one of them in anger struck me on the face with his fist; a Frenchman being by, who spoke to him some words, and went his ways; soon after came the captain of the place to the wigwam, with about twelve armed men, and asked where the Indian was that struck the Englishman, and seizing him, told him, he should go to the Bilboes, and then be hanged: The Indians were much terrified at this, as appeared by their countenance and trembling; I would have gone away too, but the Frenchman bid me not fear, the Indians durst not hurt me.

When that Indian was gone, I had two masters still, I asked them to carry me to that captain, that I might speak in behalf of the Indian; they answered, I was a fool, did I think the Frenchmen were like the English, to say one thing and do another? they were men of their words; but at length I prevailed with them to help me thither, and speaking to the captain by an interpreter, told him, I desired him to set the Indian free, declaring how kind he had been to me; he replied, he was a rogue, and should be hanged; then I privately alleged, that if he were hanged, it might fare the worse with the English captives; the captain said, that ought to be consider'd, whereupon he set him at liberty, upon condition he should never strike me more, and bring me every day to his house to eat victuals; I perceived the common people did not approve of what the Indians acted against the English: When he was free, he came and took me about the middle, saying, I was his brother, I had saved his life once, and he had saved mine (he said) thrice; he then called for brandy, and made me drink, and had me away to the wigwam again: When I came there, the Indians one after another shook hands with me, and were very kind, thinking no other but I had saved the Indian's life.

Next day he carried me to the captain's house, and set me down; they gave me victuals and wine, and being left there awhile by the Indians, I shewed the captain and his wife my fingers, who were affrighted thereat, and bid me lap it up again, and send for the chirurgeon, who when he came, said, he would cure me, and dressed it: That night I was full of pain, the French were afraid I would die, five men did watch me, and strove to keep me chearful, for I was sometimes ready to faint; oft-times they gave me a little brandy.

The next day the chirurgeon came again, and dressed me, and so he did all the while I was among the French, which was from Christmas till May. I continued in this captain's house till Benjamin Wait came and my Indian master (being in want of money) pawned me to the captain for fourteen beavers, or the worth of them, by such a day; which if he did not pay, he must lose his pawn, or else sell me for one and twenty beavers; but he could get no beaver, so I was sold, and (in God's good time) set at liberty, and returned to my friends in New England again."

It fortunately happened that at this juncture, the governor of Canada had occasion to ask a favor of the English. M. Basire, a prominent merchant at Quebec, had died, and as navigation was closed by ice in the St. Lawrence, there were no means of communicating this intelligence to his business partners in Europe, but through some port in the English colonies. The opportunity was thus offered for an interchange of civilities and mutual professions of "distinguished consideration."

On the return of the agents and the ransomed captives, they were furnished with an escort of eleven men, and set out on the 19th of April, 1678, traveling leisurely, stopping to hunt as occasion required, and occupying sixteen days in crossing the lake. Two days more brought them across the portage to the Hudson, and on the 22d of May they arrived safely in Albany. From this place Stockwell addressed a letter to his wife, announcing their safe return thus far, and on the next day again wrote, urging his friends to come on and meet the party, and to "stay not for sabbath or shoeing of horses."

Intelligence of the safe arrival and probable success of the agents, had been received at Albany in February, and doubtless became known at Hatfield, soon after. The company tarried at Albany from Wednesday till Monday, when they set out on foot, and at Kinderhook, about twenty miles distant, were relieved by horses that had been sent forward upon receiving news of their approach.

At Westfield they were met by their friends and neighbors, and their passage homeward was nothing short of a triumphal procession. Every neighborhood turned out to welcome the returning captives, and, shared with enthusiasm in the general rejoicing.[1]

Five of the French escort went on with the party, and continued their journey to Boston, having business with the government respecting some of their nation who were said to have been brought into that port as prisoners. The other six of the escort remained in Albany awaiting the return of their companions, and were meanwhile enjoying the hospitalities of the town. The commandant improved this opportunity by prying into the resources and condition of the Canadians, and comforted himself with the hope that the colony of Massachusetts would reimburse the expenses which this hospitality involved. This subject subsequently became a theme of unpleasant recrimination, as it may have been one of unavailing regret.

At the May term of the general court of Massachusetts, the governor and magistrates reported the return of the agents with the captives, and stated that great charges would arise for their redemption. They commended the case to the people of the several towns, and invited them to contribute to the fund. Anthony Stottard, John Joyliffe, and Captain John Richards, were appointed trustees to receive contributions, and the sum of three hundred and forty-five pounds, one shilling, and four pence, was raised from forty-six towns and places. Boston gave one hundred and nine pounds

[1] *Hoyt's Indian Wars*, 146; *Hubbard's Gen. Hist. N. E.*; *Holland's West. Mass.*, i, 135.

and a fraction, Portsmouth twenty pounds, Dover eleven, Charlestown fifteen, and Cambridge thirteen. It is remarked that the Isle of Shoals gave more than Salem, Kitteny as much as Lynn, Ipswich more than Charlestown, and Hull as much as Andover, Gloucester, Topsfield or Salisbury.[1]

---

[1] *Drake's Hist. Boston*, 431.

ATTACK

UPON

HATFIELD AND DEERFIELD.

PAPERS.

Letter from Major John Pynchon[1] to Captain Sylvester Salisbury.

[New York Colonial MSS., XXVI.]

[Addressed: "These ffor his Honored ffriend Capt Salisbury: Commander in Chiefe at ffort Albany. Hast. Post hast. for his Maties Special Service."]

Springfield Octobr 5th 1677

Capt Salisbury

Worthy Sr Yestarday Morning I Recd yor kind

---

[1] The writer of this letter came to Springfield when but ten years of age, and grew up with interests and sympathies closely identified with those of the frontier settlers. He became a prominent actor in the public measures of the day, and his name occurs in connection with many Indian purchases and other transactions at Springfield, and among the other river towns. He was on almost every commission and committee, was a magistrate in the local courts from the age of twenty-six till his death, and spent the greater part of his life actively and usefully employed in the public service. For a considerable period he was the chief in command of the military force of the county, was repeatedly

lines by Benja Waite,[1] whereby I vnderstand yor sympathy with vs in o^r^ sad disaster by ye Indians; & yor readiness in making great Inquiry & greate forwardness to do what Possible lys in yor for vs wch I haue abundant cause to acknouledge & doe most thankfully accept fr^m^ yor hands, & as to yor opinion of the Maquas being free, & assureing me of their Innocency, I doe fully concur wth yo^u^ having sattisfaction fr^m^ what yo^u^ wrot & fr^m^ Ben Waites Relation. But to put it out of all doubt, God in his p'vidence hath sent in one of 8 captivated men, Benoni Stebbings by name, wch is

chosen an assistant of the colony, was one of the council of New England in the time of Andros, and was named a councilor under the new colonial charter.

These several duties he sustained with great ability, and his name was a household word, not only in his county but throughout New England. During the long period that he sustained these trusts, he was never known to omit any opportunity of promoting the public good, or in the least suspected of preferring his own to the general welfare. Enjoying the public confidence which he so well merited to the last, loved, honored, and revered, he closed his earthly career at Springfield, in 1703, at the age of seventy-six.

His father, William Pynchon, alike the founder of Roxbury and Springfield, and one of the original patentees of Massachusetts bay, was at one period treasurer of the colony, and also held several colonial and local offices. He is known among theological writers as the author of a book containing views peculiar to himself upon certain doctrinal points. He died at Wragsbury on the Thames, in Buckinghamshire, Eng., in October, 1662, aged about seventy-two. The Pynchon family residence, the first brick structure in the valley, was erected in 1662, and torn down in 1831. Its picture is preserved in the seal of the city of Springfield.—*Holland's West. Mass.*, i, 144, 162; *Bradford's New Eng. Biog.*, 344; *Young's Chron. of Mass.*, 283; *Farmer's Genea. Reg.; Mass. Rec.* (*Passim*); *Mass. Hist. Coll.*, xvi, 308; *ib.*, xviii, 228, 249; *ib.*, xxviii, 248, 288, 294, *&c.* ED.

[1] From this it appears that Waite repaired to Albany immediately after the attack upon Hatfield, probably to ascertain whether the assailants were Mohawks. The opinion at first prevailed that they were such, but this was soon settled by the return of Stebbins.

y^n occasion of these lines to y^rselfe by Post, to give yo^u an $acco^t$ thereoff & to desire yo^u to put y^e Maquas vpon ꝑsucing their & our Enymys there being greate likelyhood of y^e Maquas overtaking y^m.

Benoni Stebbings came in to Hadly last night in y^e night, whose relation was sent to me wch being but an houre since I had it, I ꝑsently resolved vpon sending Post to yo^u. Take his relation as followeth. The company of Indians was Twenty only about sixe or 7 squas made 26, in all. They were this country Indians belonging to Nalwotogg[1] all of y^m but one a Narriganset. They came fr^o Canada 3 Months agoe, & had bin Hunting & were doubtfull whether to fall on Northampton or Hatfield, at last resolved on Hatfield & caryed away fro^m Hatfield 17 ꝑsons & 3 fro^m Deerfield, besides this man y^t is come in, so y^t they haue 20 captives wth y^m 3 of y^m being men, & all well as he says when they took y^m at Deerefield, after the Noise & Whoops were over at Deerefield, their first Inquiry was whether there were any Maqvas there abouts & vpon Information y^t some had been there, & were supposed not to be far off, they were all husht, & startled & greately afraid & goeing silently away forth w^{th}, they tooke vp their Lodging at Deerefield River mouth & next day crossed ye greate River vizt Conecticot to ye east side of it, the next day crossed ye River againe, afterwards, they Passed ye River many tymes having cannoes wherein they carryed ye women & children being about 2 days Journey above Squakheag,[2] they sent a company of y^m about halfe of y^m to

---

[1] Norwalk. A name evidently intended to be the same as this, is mentioned in Stebbins's narrative, on a subsequent page of this book. ED.

[2] Northfield.

Nashaway,[1] to call of some Indians yt haue bin there all this tyme of ye war & took this Benoni Stebbings along wth ym thither.[2] Coming to Nashaway Ponds, there were 3 Indian men & about halfe a score of squaws wth there children these they went too to take along wth ym having travelled from ye company they left 2 days to Squakheag & then from Squakheag somewhat more than thirty miles to ym Indians neere Nashaway who Pluckt up their stakes having Plenty of fish especially eeles, & many dryed huckleberrys but no corne: This Benoni being sent wth 2 women to carry Huccle berrys; Ran away from them, & was ꝑsently ꝑsued by some men & at one tyme was but a swamp betweene ym but night comeing on he escaped from his ꝑsuers: He says yt one of ye Indians yt they had from about Nashaway Ponds, semes to be a counsellor, & wth him they consulted much & spake of sending to ye English, but a last resolved for Canada yet talkt of making a forte a greate way vp the River & abiding there this winter, talked also of carying the captives to ye French & selling ym to ye French which he concludes they resolved on, but make but slow Passage, having so many women & children: He concluded it would be, it may be, 20 days er they get to ye Lake hunting by ye way. It was Tuesday morning last that he escaped from ye ꝑty wch caryed him with them nere Nashaway, & they had above 30 miles to goe back to Squakheag, & then neere 2 d. Journey

---

[1] Nashua was the earliest settlement in the southern part of New Hampshire, and was incorporated in 1673. During Philip's war it was abandoned. ED.

[2] Alluding to the visit made to Wanalancet of Naamkeke, who removed on the same day that Hatfield was attacked. ED.

more to ye rest above Squakheag: Ye way he says vp this River is vnpassable for English men & their goeing is by Barken cannoes much of ye way & then to ye best side of ye River men foote it leaving ye worst way: The unpassableness of ye way this way renders it vnpossible for us to ꝑsue or doe any good: But ye conveying speedy word to ye Maquas gives not only a Possibility but a ꝑbability of their overtaking ym wch Deare Sr is ye end of these lines to you; To request you (if none of ye Maqua Sachems be at Albany) to send at or charge to ye Chiefe of ye Maqvas, & give ym an accot of matters, & desire their speedy ꝑsueing these Bloody Villains & enymys of ym & forthwith & without any delay, by which meanes I hope this Barbarous Crew (who are enemys to Religion Civillity & all humanity & haue so deepely Imbrued their hands in most Innocent Blood) may be met wth in their returne, before they come to ye Lake or at ye Lake & so or captives Recovered for wch we shall give ye Maques suitable rewards. Good Sr put forward ye Maques to surprise & cut of these villaines. Let ym know yt it will be a greate demonstration of their fidelity & friendship to vs & it is a very Lukey opportunity for ym to kill & catch Indians whom they so much hunt after. And this man yt is come hom says they dread Maquas, & all their feare was least some Maquas should ꝑsue ym they did not expect or think yt English could, & desired to get out of ye Maquas way at first goeing off frm Deerefield & thinkeing they were got high enough vp from them . . . . . . a little ye more secure & at rest: so yt now I beleeve they are at ease & will make so slow ꝑgress having beside or women & children a ꝑsell of their owne women & children to clogg ym yt they may safely be taken And the lighting upon & destroying this company of ye enemy (being as it is said 17 men y^{t} is come in ye remaining strength of this River Indians) will be a breaking Blow to y^{m} & a greate meanes of o^{r} security I Pray s^{r} doe what yo^{u} can to Ingage ye Maqvas to goe out forthwith to deale effectually in it we desire to do o^{r} duty & to waite for ye salvation of God:

S^{r} excuse my scribling I am in great hast to send away ye Messenger to Westfield this Night: bee the speed in getting ye Maques to goe out upon ye Enymy before they get on ye Lake is all in all: If they can but come vp with y^{m} it will be easy to take y^{m}: for I tell yo^{u} their strength as ye man relates, & how they are clogged wth women & children I doubt not of yor helpfullness in this exigence wch will abundantly Ingage vs & wth greate Readyness shall sattisfie what ye disburse: Wth my endeared Love & Respects to yo^{u} commending yo^{u} to y^{e} ꝑtection of ye Almighty God, I remaine S^{r}

Yo^{r} very Loving ffriend & servant

JOHN PYNCHON.

Ben Waite is gon home before this Intelligence cam to me. He talkt of goeing to Canada before & I suppose will rather be forward to it now then Backward. Posible he may be at Albany about a fortnight hence in referance to a going to ye French when if I be not gon to Boston (wch I have some thoughts to doe next weeke) I shall have some opportunity againe to write to yo^{u} Vale.

J. P.

Narrative of Benoni Stebbins.

[New York Colonial MSS., xxv.]

Benonie Stebbins which was taken captive by the Indians at Dearfield 12 miles from Hatfield related as followeth

That the Indians that took him weare al Norwooluck[1] Indians saue only one which was a Naraganset. They were 26 in al 18 of them fighting men the rest 2 squas old men & boys. They told him that they had liued at the French & intended to return there again to sel the captiues to them wch had Incouradged them that they should haue eight pound ₰ peece for them and the french Indians did intend to come wth them the next time either in the spring or in winter if they had suceses this time.

The manner of his escape was thus When they came 2 days journey aboue Squakheag they sent part of their company to Wotchuset hills to fetch away 2 smal compeny of Indians that had liued there al this war time with whom they sent this captiue he being sent with 2 squas and a mare to fetch some hucleberies a litle way from the company when he got vpon the mare and rid till he tired the mare & then run on foot & so escaped to Hadly, being 2 days & ½ wthout victuals.

This relation was taken from his mouth at Northampton 6th Instant

P M SAMLL EELLS.

---

[1] Norwalk, see page 53, ante. ED.

Letter from Governor Frontenac of Canada to Governor Andros of New York.[1]

[New York Colonial MSS., xxvi.]

[Endorsed "A Copie of a Letter dated No. 18th 1677 from the Governo^r^ of Canada, to the Governor of N. Y. A Copie of another Jan 8, following."]

From Quebec, the 18th day of 9^br^ 1677.

Sr Sending now to Boston, to bee informed concerning some Frenchmen, who we heare have beene carryed Prisoners there, I was willing to take advantage of this occasion, to give you new assurances of my service, & of the good correspondence, which I desire to keepe with you.

If in that I follow the orders of the king my master, I also at the same time, satisfy my particular Inclinacon to let you know with how much truth & passion I am

Yo^r^ thrice humble servant

FRONTENAC.

Superscription as below.

From Quebec the 8th Jan 1678.

Sr The death of Mr Basire one of the principall negotiato^rs^ of this place, obliging mee to give speedy

---

[1] Sir Edmond Andros, at this period governor of New York, received in the autumn of 1677, a letter from the Duke of York, granting him permission to visit England during the winter. Upon consulting with the members of the general court of assizes, at their session in October, the condition of the colony was deemed sufficiently settled to justify his absence, and he accordingly sailed on the 17th of November. The government in the meantime devolved upon Anthony Brockholls, until the governor's return in the following summer. ED.

notice thereof to his partners in France, I thought the way of the Manhatans or Boston to bee the speediest, & the good correspondence that you have allwayes manifested a desire to entertaine betweene us makes me hope that you will direct those I shall send, the best way to have my Letters carryed into old England to be sent over from thence by the first vessells. I desire then s[r] that favo[r] of you & that you will beleeue that if in Returne, I were capable of rendring you service in these parts, I would doe it with as much joy as I am with passion,

S[r] Your servant, thrice
humble
FRONTENAC.

To Mons[r] the General Major
Andros, Goveno of New York
at Manath.

Extract from the Council Minutes.

[Council Minutes, iii, Part 2, p. 176.]

At a Councell No. 10th 1677.

Lett[rs] from Albany by Claes Luck who brought down two Englishmen that were sent from the Gov. of Boston to Albany & Canada.

Benjamin Waite owne of the two men sent downe being called in and examined what there businesse was at Albany saith that they were sent by their Mast[rs] towards Canada and had directions to goe to Albany and brought a lett[r] from the Governor of Boston to Cap[t] Salisbury, they went that way to avoyd their enemies. Being demanded of the discourse between them and some at Schanectade they saying that place did belong to Boston, the wch he denyes pretending it some mistake, they not understanding one anothers Language.

Being askt why they went away without comming againe when Capt Salisbury ordered them to come, s^d they were not willing to be hindred but to make the best of their Journey.

Stephen genning the other being askt why they went away without speaking againe to Capt Salisbery as he bad them.

He saith they were sent by the $Governo^r$ of Boston towards Canada & had orders to come by Albany, and that Capt Salisbury gave them no encouragement whereupon being desirous to follow their directions, hopeing to finde their wives and Children, they went on their Journey. Denyes saying Schanectade did belong to Boston &c but says they not understanding on another well Might Mistake.

The Matter being taken into consideracon

Resolved, that they be permitted to proceed on their voyage wch way they shall think proper, for wch order to bee sent to the Commander at Albany.

Letter from Timothy Cooper to Major John Pynchon.

[New York Colonial MSS., xxvii.]

[Endorsed: "Copie of a Lett^{r} from Mr Tim^{o} Cooper to Majo^{r} Pinchon sent doune by Capt Salisbury: Capt^{t} Salisbury writt so by order of Councell Mar. 18 1677."]

Albany ffebry 14th 167$\frac{7}{8}$

Most Worthy Majo^{r}

Sr Having now this occasion by two french from Canady who arryved here the 14th Instant beeing about 12 dayes since they cam from Canaday & now bound for Boston, I were willing to imbrace the occation knowing it my duty not to omitt any opportunity whereby I may in som small measur Maniefest the great desyer I allwayes have to serve yor worshipp to the utmost of my Capacity: having no other way at present to expresse the same then the presenting you wth these few lynes, whereby to Informe you wee have by these ffrench Intelligence of Benjamen Wait and the oy^{rs} Save arryvell att Canada: and also thar wyves & children restored unto y^{m}, the rest y^{t} were Living are redeemed from under the Indians, ther is three of the Companie dead that is 2 children & the old man the oy^{r} are all in good heallth: Benj: Waitt, and the oy^{r}, have vndergon much Trobule, & hard ship great pairt of which I will not say, it was only to satisfie some base minded persones. Though it hath now pleased God, to mak up all the Trobles they have met wth by restoring to them thar wyves, & children.

I pray God, thay May find more favo^r^, and Civell respect, from the peopell they are now among, then they have in some oy^r^ plac, of which I conclud you have already hard, and therfor at present I shall not relait to you the Cercumstance and Maner of ther vsage. But it was such as I think it fare below Christianity, or common Civility. S^r^ I begg yor pardon In what I omitt, in reference to oy^r^ Concernes, not having tym, to Inlarge, at present; But assure you, I am not unmyndfull of my Trust, but shall Indevo^r^ wth Gods assistance to discharge the same, to the good satisfaction of all. So with my humble service to yor self & good Lady, I take Leave to style my self S^r^

Yo^r^ Most humble & obedient
Servt TIMO: COOPER
Subscribitur

Passport of Monsieur Lusigny.

[New York Colonial MSS., xxvii.]

[Endorsed: "Copie of the Governo^r^ of Canada's Passeport for Monsr Lusigny who conveyed the English prison^rs^ taken by the Indians at Hadley, Hattfield &c. Apr 30th 1678."]

Le Compte de Frontenac Gouverneur et Lievte Gnall Pour sa Ma^ti^ en Canida, Accadie, Isle Terreneuve, et autres pais de la Nouvelle France.

Nousz avon donné congé et passeport au S^r^ de Lūsignij, l'un de nos Gentilshommes domestiques a qui nouz avons donne le Commandement de Lescorte des Prisonniers Anglois, faiter par Les Sacoquis que nouvs ranvoions pour aller a Orange, et de là á Boston, negotier aupres de Monsieur le gouverneur Les affaires dont nous L'avoner chargé, Ordonnons a tous ceux sur oui nostre pouvoir sistend et Prions tous autres de Laisser seureme et Libreme passer Led^{e} Sr de Lusigny avec Lescorte et les anglois quil conduit saner le faire aucun trouble nij empescheme mais au Contraire, leur donner toute sorte d'aide faveur et assistance. En Temoin de . . nous avons Signe Lejnt Passeport a ici luy fait poses Le Cachet de nos armes et contresigner Par lun de nos Secret^{res} a Quebec le trente avril mil six soix^{te} dix huit

Subscribitus,

FRONTENAC

Par Monseigneur BARROIS.

Translation.

"The Count de Frontenac, Governor and Lieutenant General for His Majesty in Canada, Acadia, Newfoundland and other territories of New France.

We have given leave and passport to Sieur de Lusigny, one of the gentlemen of our household, to whom we have entrusted the command of an escort of English prisoners taken by the Sacoquis, and whom we send back, to go to Albany and Boston to negotiate with his Honor the Governor the business with which we have charged him. We command all those within our jurisdiction, and request all others, to allow the said Sieur de Lusigny with the escort and the English whom they conduct to pass without hindrance and to render them every aid and assistance.

In witness whereof we have signed this passport, sealed it with our arms and countersigned it by one of our secretaries at Quebec this thirtieth day of April, 1678

FRONTENAC

By M. BARROIS."

Military Strength of Canada, in 1678.[1]

[New York Colonial MSS., xxvii.]

[Endorsed: "A Relacon of the forces at Canada from one of the French men in May 1678."]

Being in a discourse wth Monsr de la Chambre, (one of Count de Frontenacs Guards) did relate that they had 25 men Office^rs^ & all in the Garrison of Quebec & 33 Guns in the ffort, & in the Battery that is below the ffort, whereof 4 of the biggest (of 9^lb^ bullit) were not mounted; At troy Rivers,[2] some very few Gunns & 6 men with a serjeant, At Mont Royall[3] likewise a small Fort wth 8 men, both Townes having Gov^rs^ placed by Frontenac:

There are 6 or 8 Cap^ts^ belonging to the place, who have the Comand upon occasion of the Companyes belonging to the Colonye wch are roused in time of warre & are to bee in redinesse. The Fort at Quebec is not now strong the opening the Bastions being bloune up wth powder last St Johns day, with the losse of 9 men, & is not yet built up. He sayes they have not a strong Fort in Canada, but the Fort Cadarachque[4] is strong:

The Go: Frontenac hath some 8 or 10 Gent^l^ who

---

1 The resources of Canada were reported by M. du Chesneau to M. de Seignelay the minister, on the 10th of November, 1679, as follows:

"The general census gave 9,400 persons, of whom 515 were in Acadia; 21,900 arpens of land under cultivation, 6,983 horned cattle, 145 horses, 719 sheep, 33 goats, and 12 asses. Of firearms there were reported 1,840 guns, and 159 pistols."—*N. Y. Col. Doc.*, ix, 136. ED.

2 Three Rivers. ED.

3 Montreal. ED.

4 Cataraqui, now Kingston. ED.

doe keepe him Comp^{a}, and doe eate at his Table daily, he hath 16 men to bee his Guard & all other officers in his house, as our Earles have in Engl^{d} this is what I have learnt at present having not yet fully discoursed with him, the rest you shall have ℘ the next.

Letter from Capt. Salisbury to Capt. Brockholls.

[New York Colonial MSS., xxvii.]

Sr Upon the 22th of this Instant came to this Place Benjamin Wayt & Stephen Gennings with 19 of those people y^{t} were taken by ye Indians at Hadfeilde & Hadly & have for there convoy 11 ffrench men 3 of them belonge to ye Gov^{e} of Cannada garde & those 3 with other 2 goeth with those people to Boston. The other 6 staye heere untill ye 5 doeth come backe hauing passes & letrs of credence, and to detaine them I coulde not see any strength to doe it, therefore I desire you'l spedy answer by this expresse, wheather I shall detaine them & sende them down at there Returne for I woulde be punctiall in my Dewty, and not willing to committ any Errors, soe yor spedy answer of my Laste as well as of this will be a very greate help to let me see how I shall Govern myselfe.

I haue Descoursed with Benja Wayte Consarning there lineing in Canada & how strong in men & in there ffortifycations & as to there lineing its very meaine for the Commonallity are very much oppresed with greate taxes, but the Gou^{r} and ye reste of the greate ones, lines hy after the French manner and so there strenth of men thay cane make 1000 or 2 but thay line in littell villages haueing littell plantations here & there som 20 & 30 miles from villadge to villadge & in som vil there is 20 & some 30 houses. They liue as Indians and gett there lineing by hunteing and there fortifications ar not very stronge. I woulde know wheather I shall beare there Expences while there aboad is heer & I pray you let the bearers be furnished with prouitions at ther Returne haueing not ffurther to inlarge but remaine your very humble serv[t]

SILVES' SALISBURY.

ffort Albany y[e] 23th May 1678.

Letter from Capt. Brockholls to Capt. Salisbury.

[New York Colonial MSS., xxvii.]

Cap[t] Salisbury.

S[r] I recd yo[rs] Yesterday in the Evening of the 23th with the enclosed copies of passeports & Letter from the Governo[r] of Canada, wherein you intimate the coming of 11 French men to Albany to convey Benjamin Wait & Stephen Gennings with the people that were taken prisoners by the Indyans the last fall at Hatfield & Hadley (who without doubt are joyfull to returne back to their habitacons) withall that 5 of the 11 French were gone forward to Boston with those people, the other 6 remaining behind with you untill the returne of their Comerades concerning y[e] carriage to whom you desire to bee advised I have comunicated what you writ & . . . . . Councell who are of opinion that [there was] no need to have conveyed those [men farther] than Albany, from whence you might [have sent] persons with them to their homes.

The Comunicacon of the French with the Indyans

as they passe being to bee suspected, at that time of so great a likelyhood of warrs with them and it would haue beene well to have knowne what buisnesse they had to negotiate with the Go: of Boston, but since they are past it cannot bee helpt & it is hoped they will doe no greate harme & there being as yet no declaracon of warre knowne to [have been made and their] coming also upon so charitable an Acc^{t} as the Redemption & bringing back of poore distrested captives of our nation I know not well upon w^{t} pretence they could bee stopt, so that it is therefore the opinion of the Counsell, that when the other 5 shall bee returned back you use them with all civility & permitt them quietly to returne back to Canada about their occasions. As for their Expences at Albany it is likewise thought fitt that you defray them for the present & that they be cleared from it onely that you take [account of the expense] & send it hither where care will bee taken [to send] it to the Go: of Boston, who ought to allow [the amount] it being for people of his Governm^{t}. There was an answer went yesterday to the Comissioners of Alb. before the receit of this concerning the buisnesse of Will Teller[1] & Will Loveredge with what else was written about by them.

Yo^{r} Messenger being dispatcht returnes this afternoone Having not farther I remaine S^{r} yor very humble serv^{t} A. B.

N. Y. Sunday May 26. 1678.

---

[1] Charged with accidental homicide of an Indian, and released May 20. Ed.

Letter from Count Frontenac to Capt. Brockholls, without date; received May 31, 1678.

[N. Y. Colonial MSS., xxvii.]

Sr The letter you did mee the hono^r to write mee of the 28th of February last, is so civill & the offers you make mee so obliging, that I am glad the sending back of the English taken prison^rs by the Indyans, (who I caused to be conducted to Orange) hath furnisht me with an opportunity to returne you my thanks sooner than I expected.

I understood by the persons I sent to Boston as also by the Letters from Go Leverett & the councell, that the Frenchmen sent to enquire after were releast, & by that from Capt Salisbury that Go: Andros arrived well at London in 5 weekes time. I wish him a returne as happy & that I may find means to shew both to him & you the desire I always haue to hold a good correspondence in testifying both to the one & the other how much I am,

S^r Yo^r thrice humble serv^t

FRONTENAC.

Letter from Capt. Brockholls to Count Frontenac.

[N. Y. Colonial MSS., xxvii; Translated from the French.]

Sir. I have received yours by the hands of William Davy and Peter Monteray, two of your people who accompanied Captain de Lusigny to Albany on his way to restore the English taken prisoners by the Indians to their families and friends.

Your great kindness in the redemption of these poor unfortunates out of the hands of their enemies merits great praise and gratitude from all Christians and may God reward you for it. I have charged your people to return for me many thanks for the obliging and generous civilities which you were pleased to express in your letter.

We have received letters from Mr Andros our Governor at London, in which he states that he will soon return, so that we expect him daily. The desire you express for a friendly correspondence shall be reciprocated on our part, and if in any thing I may be able to render you service I shall have the pleasure of showing how much I am

Your very humble & obedient servt

A. B.

New York June 6, 1678.

INDEX.

CPSIA information can be obtained
at www.ICGtesting.com
Printed in the USA
LVHW111509230223
740229LV00002B/77

9 783382 302955